DOLPHINS SET II

STRIPED DOLPHINS

Kristin Petrie

ABDO Publishing Company

visit us at
www.abdopub.com

Published by ABDO Publishing Company, 4940 Viking Drive, Edina, Minnesota 55435.
Copyright © 2006 by Abdo Consulting Group, Inc. International copyrights reserved in all
countries. No part of this book may be reproduced in any form without written permission from
the publisher. The Checkerboard Library™ is a trademark and logo of ABDO Publishing
Company.

Printed in the United States.

Cover Photo: © Doug Perrine / SeaPics.com
Interior Photos: © Doug Perrine / SeaPics.com pp. 8, 10, 13, 14-15, 17, 21; © Joao Quaresma /
    SeaPics.com p. 5; Peter Arnold p. 19; Uko Gorter pp. 6-7

Series Coordinator: Megan M. Gunderson
Editors: Heidi M. Dahmes, Megan M. Gunderson
Art Direction, Diagram, & Map: Neil Klinepier

Library of Congress Cataloging-in-Publication Data

Petrie, Kristin, 1970-
    Striped dolphins / Kristin Petrie.
        p. cm. -- (Dolphins. Set II)
    Includes index.
    ISBN 1-59679-304-X
    1. Striped dolphin--Juvenile literature. I. Title.

QL737.C432P467 2005
599.53'4--dc22

                                                            2005048109

CONTENTS

STRIPED DOLPHINS 4

SIZE, SHAPE, AND COLOR 6

WHERE THEY LIVE 8

SENSES 10

DEFENSE 12

FOOD 14

BABIES 16

BEHAVIORS 18

STRIPED DOLPHIN FACTS 20

GLOSSARY 22

WEB SITES 23

INDEX 24

STRIPED DOLPHINS

All dolphins are mammals. This means they are warm-blooded. Mammals are born with hair, and they nurse their young with milk. Dolphins can be many different sizes and colors. Some are found only in rivers. Others are found in oceans throughout the world.

Striped dolphins are part of the Delphinidae **family**. This is the largest family of **cetaceans**. The scientific name for striped dolphins is *Stenella coeruleoalba*. The *Stenella* **genus** includes more individuals than any other genus of dolphins.

Striped dolphins are famous for their **streamlined** look. Like a hot rod car, their racing stripes streak from head to tail. Striped dolphins also act cool. They put on a great show with somersaults and dives. Striped dolphins can jump 23 feet (7 m) out of the water!

The second half of the striped dolphin's scientific name describes its color. *Coeruleoalba* means "sky blue" and "white."

Size, Shape, and Color

Striped dolphins are medium-sized dolphins. Males can reach nearly nine feet (3 m) in length. And, females can reach nearly eight feet (2.5 m). On average, striped dolphins weigh 200 to 350 pounds (90 to 160 kg).

The striped dolphin has a robust, **streamlined** body. It starts with a relatively long snout. Down the back is a tall, dark **dorsal** fin with a sharp tip. A narrow flipper projects from each side. And, the striped dolphin's body ends with powerful **flukes**.

FLUKE

The striped dolphin has distinctive coloring. The pattern is not only different in each region of the world, but also on each dolphin. The striped dolphin's belly is white. And, each dolphin has a dark band of color on its head and back that looks like a cape!

The striped dolphin has narrow, black stripes on each side of its body. The longest stripe starts just behind each eye. It streaks all the way to the dolphin's tail. A second, smaller stripe goes around each eye. It ends just before each flipper.

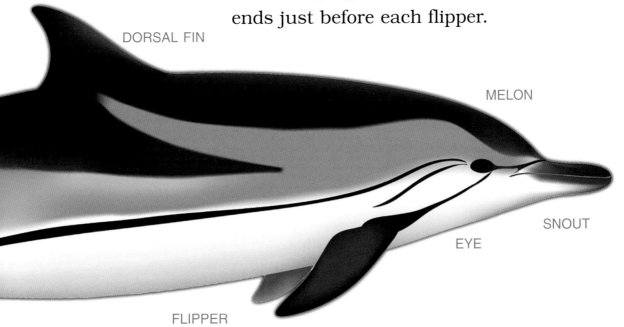

DORSAL FIN

MELON

SNOUT

EYE

FLIPPER

WHERE THEY LIVE

Striped dolphins call the Atlantic, Pacific, and Indian oceans home. They also live in the Mediterranean and Caribbean seas. And, they are found in the northern Gulf of Mexico.

Their **habitat** is limited only by water temperature. You won't find striped dolphins near the North Pole! These dolphins prefer tropical or **temperate** water. They like the surface water to be at least 72 degrees Fahrenheit (22°C).

Striped dolphins usually migrate to follow warm, shifting ocean currents.

Striped dolphins are mainly an oceanic mammal. This means they stick to deep parts of the ocean. So, they are usually found no closer to land than the **continental shelf**. They are also not known to **migrate** very far.

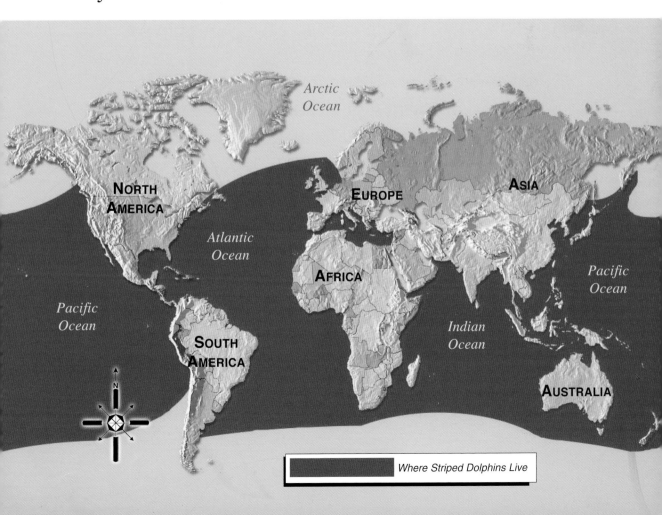

Where Striped Dolphins Live

SENSES

You may have heard that dolphins make a lot of noise. If you guessed that they were talking, then you were right. Many dolphins sing, whistle, and make clicking noises to communicate.

Sometimes, dolphins use noises for more than communication. With a process called echolocation, dolphins turn sound into information. For example, the noise a dolphin sends out may bounce off objects in the water. Then, it returns to the dolphin to be processed.

These echoes tell a dolphin many things. Echolocation can help dolphin species avoid

Scientists study communication and echolocation sounds to learn more about each dolphin species.

10

predators and other dangers. The sound may bounce off a ship. This tells the dolphin to get out of the way! Or, the noise may hit a school of fish. This tells the dolphin that food is near.

Sound wave sent out by dolphin

Echo wave received by dolphin

DEFENSE

Many dolphin species have natural **predators** such as killer whales or sharks. But for striped dolphins, humans are the main danger. Fishing causes the most harm to striped dolphins. And, the dolphins have little defense against this threat.

Fishing nets are hard to avoid because they are big and hard to see. Plus, they hold all kinds of fish that dolphins want to eat! Unfortunately, there is no easy way out of these fishing nets. Thousands of striped dolphins die each year from becoming tangled in them.

Fishing nets harm striped dolphins in other ways, too. In certain areas, too many schooling fish are taken. Overfishing affects the food chain in a **habitat**. Along with pollution, overfishing can cause dolphins and other sea life to be left hungry.

Water pollution can make a dolphin more likely to get a disease.

Luckily, there are many striped dolphins. The worldwide population is not known, but scientists believe they are thriving. Still, there is reason for concern. In some areas, striped dolphins are hunted for their meat. In other areas, disease has killed many.

FOOD

The striped dolphin's diet often depends on where in the world it lives. Like many dolphin species, the striped dolphin eats fish. Any kind of schooling fish attracts the striped dolphin. However, its favorite food is squid.

A dolphin's diet depends on its habitat. So, a striped dolphin in the Mediterranean Sea may eat different foods than one in the Atlantic Ocean.

Striped dolphins will dive to great depths to find food. If squid are not available, striped dolphins will feed on a variety of prey. These include **crustaceans** such as shrimps and crabs. They even eat lantern fish, which glow in the dark!

Striped dolphins work together when hunting. They will even hunt with other fish, such as tuna. Striped dolphins have 39 to 55 pairs of teeth in both their upper and lower jaws. These teeth help them catch their food.

BABIES

Striped dolphins begin reproducing at 7 to 15 years of age. This is when they have grown to about seven feet (2 m). Scientists believe mating occurs in summer and winter. But, mating rituals are a mystery since these dolphins stay far from shore.

Mother striped dolphins are **pregnant** for about 12 to 13 months. They give birth to one baby about every three to four years. Baby dolphins are called calves. Striped dolphin calves are about 40 inches (100 cm) long at birth. And, they weigh 15 to 24 pounds (7 to 11 kg).

Calves stay close to their mother. They are nursed with their mother's milk for about 16 months. One to two years after **weaning**, many calves leave their mother's **pod**. They go in search of a younger crowd. Striped dolphins can live for 58 years.

Most calves spend their early years in pods composed of at least 30 adults, young dolphins, and other calves.

BEHAVIORS

Striped dolphins usually live in **pods** of 100 dolphins. But at times, there may be up to 3,000 dolphins together. In these crowds, up to 1,000 dolphins may be jumping at one time.

Striped dolphins are extremely active. They love somersaulting, tail spinning, **bow riding**, and **breaching**. They are impressive underwater, too. Striped dolphins make deep dives of up to 650 feet (200 m). They may stay underwater for five to ten minutes.

Striped dolphins are speedy swimmers. They can cruise at up to 23 miles per hour (37 km/h). At this speed, they leap at the ocean's surface about every five seconds. With their capelike color pattern, striped dolphins look like they are flying!

Disease killed more than 1,000 Mediterranean striped dolphins in the early 1990s. So, the average pod size in that region was only seven. Today, the pods in that region are back to an average of 25 dolphins.

STRIPED DOLPHIN FACTS

Scientific Name: *Stenella coeruleoalba*

Common Names: Whitebelly, Blue-White Dolphin, Meyen's Dolphin, Gray's Dolphin, Streaker Porpoise, Euphrosyne Dolphin

Average Size: Males reach a maximum size of nearly nine feet (3 m). Females are slightly smaller, reaching a maximum of nearly eight feet (2.5 m). This species can weigh 200 to 350 pounds (90 to 160 kg).

Where They're Found: Tropical and temperate regions of the Atlantic, Pacific, and Indian oceans, the Mediterranean and Caribbean seas, and the northern Gulf of Mexico

Sometimes, dolphins and whales strand, or appear on a shore. This can be deadly for any species. One time, about 100 striped dolphins stranded at the same time.

GLOSSARY

bow riding - when some toothed cetaceans swim at the front of a boat or ship and use the waves created there to assist their swimming and speed.

breach - to jump or leap up out of the water.

cetacean (sih-TAY-shuhn) - any of various types of mammal, such as the dolphin, that live in water like fish.

continental shelf - a shallow, underwater plain that borders a continent and ends with a steep slope to the ocean floor.

crustacean (kruhs-TAY-shuhn) - any of a group of animals with hard shells that live mostly in water. Crabs, lobsters, and shrimps are all crustaceans.

dorsal - located near or on the back, especially of an animal.

family - a group that scientists use to classify similar plants or animals. It ranks above a genus and below an order.

fluke - either of the fins that make up the tail of a cetacean, such as a whale or dolphin.

genus - a group that scientists use to classify similar plants or animals. It ranks above a species and below a family.

habitat - a place where a living thing is naturally found.

migrate - to move from one place to another, often to find food.

pod - a group of animals, typically whales or dolphins.

predator - an animal that kills and eats other animals.

pregnant - having one or more babies growing within the body.

streamlined - having a shape that reduces the resistance to motion when moving through air or water.

temperate - having neither very hot nor very cold weather.

wean - to accustom an animal to eat food other than its mother's milk.

WEB SITES

To learn more about striped dolphins, visit ABDO Publishing Company on the World Wide Web at **www.abdopub.com**. Web sites about these dolphins are featured on our Book Links page. These links are routinely monitored and updated to provide the most current information available.

INDEX

A

Atlantic Ocean 8

C

calves 4, 16
Caribbean Sea 8
color 4, 6, 7, 18

D

defense 10, 11, 12
Delphinidae 4
diving 4, 15, 18
dorsal fin 6

E

echolocation 10, 11
eyes 7

F

flippers 6, 7
flukes 6
food 4, 11, 12, 14,
    15, 16

H

habitat 4, 8, 9, 12,
    14, 16
head 4, 7
hunting 15

I

Indian Ocean 8

L

life span 16

M

mammals 4, 9
Mediterranean Sea 8
Mexico, Gulf of 8
migration 9

P

Pacific Ocean 8
pods 16, 18
population 13
predators 11, 12

R

reproduction 16

S

senses 10, 11
size 4, 6, 16
snout 6
sounds 10, 11
speed 18

T

tail 4, 7
teeth 15
threats 11, 12, 13